DIARY OF A
NINJA SPY
4

Where evil goes, the ninja will follow...

Diary of a Ninja Spy 4: Clone Attack!

(Book 4)

William Thomas

Peter Patrick

Also by William Thomas and Peter Patrick:

Diary of a Ninja Spy

Diary of a Ninja Spy 2

Diary of a Ninja Spy 3

Diary of a Ninja Spy 5

In the Diary of a Super Spy series:

Diary of a Super Spy

Diary of a Super Spy 2: Attack of the Ninjas!

Diary of a Super Spy 3: A Giant Problem!

Diary of a Super Spy 4: Space!

Diary of a Super Spy 5: Evil Attack!

Diary of a Super Spy 6: Daylight Robbery!

Chapter 1

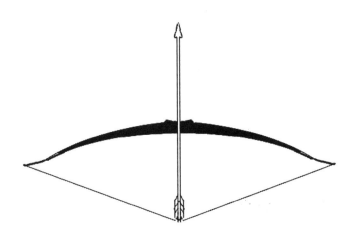

"QUIET! Alright listen up, you little stinky, smelly, reeking youngsters."

I'm pretty sure our teacher doesn't like children.

"This homework needs to be completed by tomorrow. I don't want any excuses from you! Not one!" continues Mrs. Nutty as she talks to the class. "I know that you are all silly little idiots, but this has to be completed!"

Yep, I'm fairly confident now that she doesn't like children at all.

"I don't want to hear any adventures about ninjas in our town or epic fighting battles taking place outside your houses," Mrs. Nutty rambles on.

The disturbances around the neighborhood are probably my fault, I'm still learning how to be stealthy and silent while on top secret ninja missions. Usually, I get caught up in the moment and I love to yell out cliché war cries when fighting.

For example, a few nights ago I was battling Slime Zero, a giant slug, in a take-out restaurant and I screamed out, "Would you like fries with that?" as I a-salted the slug!

Ha!

I am a one-liner genius!

But sadly, that is not the way of the Ninja Spy.

My name is Blake Turner, and I am a Ninja Spy.

I have had a lot of excitement in my life since becoming an official Ninja Spy, but it is *soooo* time consuming!

I thought it would be like the comic books - save the day quickly, bask in the glory, then go home for a nap.

But No!

It is nothing like that at all.

I train and train and train and train, then I study and study and study and study.

And when it comes to the battles, they just go on and on and on. Not one enemy of mine has given up easily and surrendered on the spot.

The fights go on for hours!

And they are **exhausting!**

All that is just part of my Ninja Spy life, I still have to live out my real identity as an ordinary school kid too.

That involves gaming, attending school and homework!

So much useless homework!

I haven't had a moment to myself since becoming an elite secret hero.

I'm not complaining, I love saving the day and destroying the bad guys, but I just wish it wasn't so demanding on my time.

"I'm really starting to struggle with this whole balancing two lives stuff," I say to my best friend Fred as we walk home together.

"My grades are slipping, and if they slip any more my parents won't let me leave the house. What am I going to do, Doodle?"

Doodle is my new, cool way of saying dude.

"Hmmmm," Fred says, "You are in a bit of trouble there, aren't you? There is only one of you."

"Thanks Einstein. I know there is only one of meeeeee... **Boom!** That's it! Fred, you are a genius!"

Chapter 2

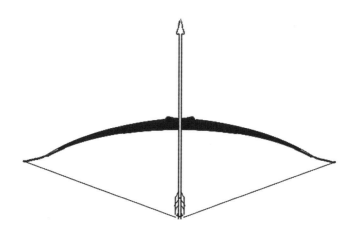

I race over to the Ninja Spy headquarters to see my comrade Agent Lightning.

She is currently testing a new Ninja Spy gadget, the Brain Understanding Measurer, or the B.U.M, for short. It is a tool that measures the size of someone's brain activity. The smarter the person, the higher the reading on the scale.

Before she tests her B.U.M. on me, I interrupt and tell her of my idea.

Well, what do you think?" I ask, already knowing what she will say - Blake, you are a genius, or something like that.

"Blake."

"Yes," I reply as I wait for my praise.

"Why do you keep talking to me? There are other Ninja Spy Agents you can talk to here. Stop harassing me."

Not the answer I was expecting. Probably just playing hard to get - I do have a crush on Agent Lightning and she knows it.

"Oh you. Agent Lightning, stop joking around."

"Grrr, who's joking?"

"Well, what about my idea? It is pretty good, uh?" I should wait around to hear her approval but I see my mentor, Tekato, sneaking through the room. I run up to him and sell my idea again.

"No, Blake. Just no. There are too many things that could go wrong."

Clearly Agent Lightning and Tekato are simply jealous of my idea.

Even though they said it was a terrible idea, I think that they meant it was a great idea.

But if they are not going to help me, the next thing I should do is go home and develop a prototype of my new idea.

"Blake, it is late, you should go to bed. Have you completed your homework?" Mom asks me as I'm crouched over a ton of papers.

My parents don't appreciate how busy my life is. They don't know that I've been saving the world outside school hours.

"I'm doing it now," I lie, pretending the paperwork is my homework.

The homework can wait, in fact it may even do itself later on!

Haha!

I've been up all night scribbling plans for my project.

I am going to build a clone!

A copy of myself!

This is going to be brilliant!

Two of me will be able to get twice as much done!

I will be able to go out and tackle all my Ninja Spy duties while my clone is stuck doing all my boring chores and school work!

I keep drafting and redrafting my plan for hours.

Suddenly, I notice the sun starting to rise!

Eeekk! I have school soon!

I haven't slept or started my homework yet!

A short time later, I am getting on the school bus.

I am *sooo* tired. So very, very tired.

I'm struggling to keep my eyes open.

My vision is blurry and I'm quite sure that my words are mumbling out of my mouth. I must look a mess. I climb up the seats of the school bus and sit next to Fred.

"Yawn,….meh Fred," I say, trying to form a sentence.

"Good morning, Blake. These late nights are taking a toll on you, aren't they?"

"Is it that obvious?" I reply drearily.

"You should stop. You need to give up the Ninja Spy work. It is too much for you to handle," Fred tries to reason with me.

"Naaahhhh, Justice. Me uphold justice. Me do good," I say as I start to doze off.

With my last motion before I collapse from a lack of sleep, I thrust my clone blueprint into Fred's hand.

"Take a look at this. It work?" I mumble my final words as I fall into a deep sleep on the school bus.

I wake up ten minutes later to find tears running down Fred's face.

"Fred, what happened? Are you ok? Who did this to you?" I question him.

"It was you."

"Whaaa?"

Quickly, I realize that Fred's tears are not from pain or hurt.

Fred was crying from laughter.

And I think I know why.

He is holding my blueprint plans for making a clone and bursting out laughing every time he glances at it.

"Blake, how long did you spend on this plan?" asks Fred.

"I was up all night," I respond.

"Really?"

"Yup, that *only* took me one night," I say proudly.

Fred shows me what I have drawn. In hindsight, my plan was missing some details.

"Blake, it is a badly drawn picture of you with a multiplication sign next to it. How did this take all night?"

I shrug.

I thought it was good.

I know the plan is missing some of the finer scientific points.

But the reason I revealed my super plan to Fred is so he can help make it.

Fred is the smartest person I know, even smarter than some of the Ninja Spies I've met at the agency. If anyone can make this work, it is Fred.

"OK, leave it with me, I'll have a look later. My school day takes primary importance," says Fred.

He is such a nerd.

"Thanks, Fred. What lesson do we have first," I ask Fred as we jump off the school bus.

"We have Mrs. Nutty first period."

I freeze. Drat. I was up all night working on my master-plan and I didn't have time for my homework. Argh!

"Fred," I say calmly.

"Yes."

"Sorry."

"Sorry, for wha..." Fred is unable to finish his sentence and falls limp, like a half zombie.

I use a special holding move on Fred that turns him limp by squeezing a few pressure points.

I know I should not be using this secret Ninja Spy move on an ordinary innocent person, but I have no choice. I can't walk into Mrs. Nutty's classroom without my homework.

I need a clone now, then they can deal with Mrs. Nutty's rage while I do something fun. I need Fred to start working on my clone ASAP!

I carry Fred back to the garden shed in my backyard.

"BLAKE!" Fred screams as he comes back to consciousness a few minutes later. "Where am I? Have you kidnapped me?!"

"No, no. It is only kidnapping if you don't want to be here," I explain.

"I don't want to be here, Blake!"

"Oh, then yes, this is a kidnapping."

"Fred, I need your help. Please? I need a clone urgently. There should be enough junk and parts in here to make a clone," I plead with Fred.

"Hmmmppp. No. I am not happy with you at all! I happen to like school, and I don't appreciate being forced away to do your science project. I am going back to school."

"Whoa, slow down there, friend. How about if I let you use my clone as well?"

"I can do my own homework, Blake."

"No, he would do something else for you. My clone could act as your bodyguard when I'm not around," I say.

Fred's incredible intelligence comes at a cost. Bullies don't like nerds. Fred is often traumatized by some of the other kids at school.

"My clone could offer you protection!"

"Hmmm," Fred is deep in thought, "Ok, let's do it. **Let's clone you!**"

Chapter 3

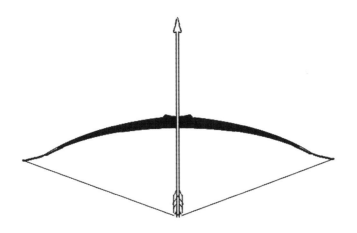

After a few hours of welding, gluing and nailing, Fred has made a cloning machine!

But it isn't as futuristic as I had hoped.

It resembles more of a junkyard project than a state of the art piece of equipment. It's a collection of mirrors, wires, shovels, picks and batteries.

"This is the best that we can do with what we have," explains Fred. "You stand in front of the mirror as I power it up. The mirror will take a picture of you and reproduce you over there, under the sprinkler head. You will also need to wear this modified bike helmet so the machine can copy your mind."

"Awesome! No more homework for me!" I yell as I put on the helmet and move into position.

As I walk across the room, I trip on a wire and it pops out of the machine.

Eeekk!

I look at it blankly because I have no idea where it came from or what it does. Fred didn't see me clumsily damaging his work, so I pretend it didn't happen.

I don't want to upset Fred after all his hard work.

Also I feel a little bad, I haven't done a single thing.

I just watched him invent a contraption while I played with some of my old toys.

"Blake, this hasn't been tested. It could be dangerous," Fred says in a concerning tone. "If any of my calculations are incorrect or a piece of the equipment doesn't function properly, who knows what will happen."

"Meh, it will be fine. Stop your stressing, Mr. Stress-head."

Hmmm, maybe I should mention the disconnected wire…

"Blake, stand still," Fred commands.

"But Fred-"

Woooooooozzzzzzzzzzzzzzzuuuuuuuuuhhhppff!

The entire shed is lit up!

As the light slowly disappears and my vision comes back, I notice my image in the mirror is gone! I turn around to tell Fred but he is punching the air in joy.

"What happened? Did it work?" I ask.

"Sure did, doodle."

Doodle? That is my thing to say! Who? I spin around to see whose voice is mimicking me.

It is me! It worked! The cloning worked! I'm staring at **myself!**

Chapter 4

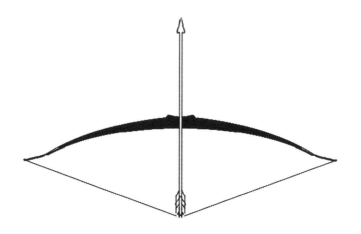

"Hello, my name is Blake," I introduce myself to myself.

"I know who you are, you moron," the clone snaps back.

"Wow, you have a bit of an attitude," chuckles Fred.

I'm not going to stand here and take that from me. I've got to assert my authority.

"I am *your* leader. You must do what I say. Do you understand? You work for me," I set out the rules to my clone.

"If I am really a clone of yours, you would know that I do not follow rules easily," replies my clone.

That is true. Have I just been outwitted by myself?

"I am the original Blake, so therefore I am the boss," I explain to the clone.

"Na-uh. I'm the new and improved model. In fact, I'm smarter than you," says my clone. "I wouldn't clone myself expecting myself to follow orders from myself. Especially if I know that I can be rebellious."

"Blake, he has a point," Fred agrees.

"Don't agree with him. Fred, you should be on my side," I say, glaring at Fred.

"I am. But on his side too. He is your clone. So I am still taking your side," Fred explains.

"Don't confuse me!"

"He is a little slow, isn't he?"

My clone just asked Fred if I'm slow! That is insulting!

"I'm just as clever as you, you banana! You are my clone, remember?"

"Nope, I'm a smarter version of you," replies my clone. "The wire that you pulled out of the machine was a very important wire. That wire was in place to transfer some of your idiotic traits to me - your clone. But as you pulled it out, I am now a little smarter than you."

"Blake!" Fred yells as he kneels down to look at the wire. "You pulled out a wire from my machine and didn't tell me?! Your clone is right! This wire was to transfer your stupidity… and your goodness. So that means your clone is smart and… evil!"

I feel as if this is going to work against me.

"He is now the more superior Blake!" barks Fred.

"Don't be mad, Fred," says my clone. "As a more intelligent Blake I will treat you better as a friend. For example, I won't kidnap you in order to get out of homework. See, I'm not *that* evil. There is no need to be worried."

I think he is lying.

"Oh, I do like the sound of that," says Fred. "Maybe I've improved you."

"No! Stop! Don't trust him – he is evil! He is here just to do my boring stuff while I go and do cool Ninja Spy stuff," I raise my voice.

"We can't trust the clone. He might want to take over the world!"

"Don't be angry, Blake. I have plenty of time to take over the world. I'll do the cool stuff for now and you focus on getting your school work done. I can tell you, you really will benefit from more school time. There is no point of me going, I know all that stuff already," says my clone.

I can't believe this! My imposter is going to lead the life I want!

"Well, guess what, Clone!? I'm still not going to go to school, so you have to," I try calling his bluff.

"That is fine, Blake," replies my clone, "I'm not the one who will get in trouble - you will. I am just the clone of you, remember?"

Wait a minute, did I just get outwitted again? I look to Fred for confirmation. He is smiling and nodding. Drat.

"One more thing, Blake," says my identical being who appears to be wittier than me, "Call me Blake."

"ARGH! No! You are a clone! **I am Blake!**"

Chapter 5

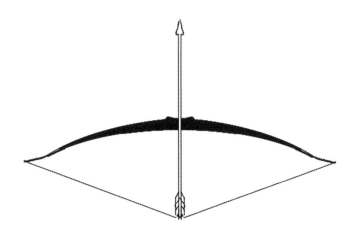

Finally, it is the weekend and I have a chance to catch up on some of my Ninja Spy chores.

I walk in the Ninja Spy H.Q. and everyone is staring at me. I'm quite sure I haven't done anything wrong. A few of the agents are smiling and nodding to me.

Hmmmm, weird.

I open up the door to the unsolved cases room and I realize why the agents are staring at me.

They think I've already walked in - standing in front of me is my clone with a big, stupid grin.

Man, I am annoying me.

"Good morning, Clone," he says.

"No! You are the clone! I am the original!" I yell.

Standing next to my clone is Agent Lightning. Actually, she is standing very close to my clone. It is as if they are… flirting!

Arghh!

My clone has hit on my crush!

And he is doing better than I am!

"I joke, I joke, Blake. You can be the original Blake. I am the new and improved Blake," says my clone. "I have told my dear friend here, Agent Lightning, about your experiment."

"Hey, stop it! You are frustrating me! That is MY dear friend!" I object to my clone's statement.

"I have changed my mind. I think your experiment was the right thing to do, Blake," says Agent Lightning.

"Really? But he is evil!"

"He's not evil," Agent Lighting disagrees. "He is really nice. I will happily work with this version of you. Look at all the filing and paperwork we have completed this morning! You had this paperwork on your desk for months, and your clone has completed it in just one morning. At this rate, we will be up to date and out to solve new cases by lunch! This is great news!"

ARGH!

I am going to explode in rage shortly!

But I must keep my mouth shut. I suck in a ton of air through my nostrils and try to calm down.

"That. Is. Great. News," I reluctantly spit out and then storm out of the room.

I thought my clone and I would be friends!

I thought we would be playing jokes on people and playing in the park together!

Instead, **I am now my own worst enemy!**

Chapter 6

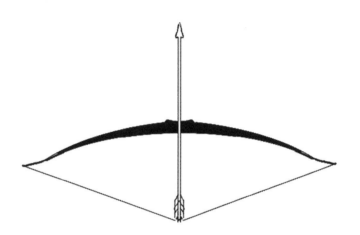

I follow the clone around the headquarters trying to see what 'an intelligent' version of me would do. As I follow him around, I notice more and more agents taking a liking to him… I mean, me.

This isn't fair!

They should have liked me before!

I feel I have outplayed myself.

Despite seeing myself succeed, I really want him to fail.

I don't want to be the one stuck at school while he runs around holding hands with Agent Lightning.

And I'm sure he is evil… he is just being nice so that he can destroy the Ninja Spy Agency from the inside out.

Looks like Evil Blake has to go.

I walk back into the room with a friendly attempt to outplay myself.

"Hey Blake," I call out. It really grinds me that I have to call him by my name. His name should be copycat or stunt double. "Could you help me in the incinerator room?"

"Sure thing, stupid version of me," he replies. I'll be glad when this smarty is gone.

The incinerator room has a giant garbage disposal unit where the Ninja Spies get rid of toxic waste.

I lead him into the incinerator room and lock the door behind us. We are the only ones in here. Now – time to destroy myself!

I throw a punch to his left, but he easily moves aside while laughing.

"Haha, Blake stop!" my clone pleads. "You can't destroy me! I'm you! I know all your moves!"

Damn, he is right.

This is going to be a very even fight.

I thrust a quick kick forward to his stomach.

But he jumps out of the way!

"I knew you would do that too."

"We are not leaving this room until you are in the blender!" I state.

"Nice try, Blake. I knew that is why you wanted to see me in here, so I disabled the incinerator before we walked in."

"No!" I have been outsmarted again.

"Maybe it is time you stood aside to let me take over your life? I'll be better at it than you. You are an idiot," my clone is heckling me. "Now leave me alone before you make an uber-smart new enemy."

"I'm going to get my life back, clone!" I scream.

I storm out of the headquarters after failing to defeat myself.

****

I take a short walk to clear my head before I go to talk with Fred. He will be able to help me. I take off my ninja uniform and knock on Fred's door.

"What do you want now?" Fred's brother answers.

"Excuse me?" I reply.

"You were just here. Fred just left with you."

Sigh, of course my clone already worked out my plan - go see Fred for help.

Give me a break! C'Mon!

As I wander back to my house, I hear some mumbles in the park. It is getting dark so I creep up slowly to see what is making the noises.

Oh-no!

It is Fred!

He is tied up to the see-saw. No one else is around.

"What are you doing here?" I ask as I rip the tape from his mouth.

"It was your clone! He has gone crazy! He really is evil! He came around to tell me that he was going to be you from now on. And that you need to be eliminated! And he wants to take over the world! I said no, that's not fair. He told me that if I'm not on his side, I'll be his enemy! Then he tied me up here!"

Oh no, I've gone mad with intelligence.

"And then he said he is going to kill all the Ninja Spies so he can rule the world! And he's going to kill Agent Lighting first! He's crazy, Blake! Crazy! We need to stop him!" Fred bellows.

It is the second time this week that Fred has been kidnapped by a Blake. Poor Fred really can only handle one Blake as a friend.

I didn't expect my day to end like this - developing a battle plan for destroying myself.

Only Fred and I know of the clone's plan to take over my life. I don't want to risk telling Agent Lightning or Tekato because I believe that he will hurt them too if they try and stop him. Even worse, they might agree that he is a better version to have around.

We retreat to my parent's garden shed to come up with a strategy to put an end to the second me.

"Fred," I jump up. "I have it. Let's fight fire with fire!"

"What do you mean?"

"Let's build more clones!"

Chapter 7

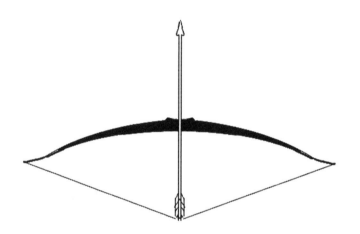

"Blake, this didn't work the first time. Only one Blake should be in this town. The other Blake is too smart and too evil. Intelligence is a dangerous ingredient when mixed with your thoughts."

"Um, thanks?" I reply, not sure if that was an insult or compliment.

Fred seems unsure of my new plan to create more copies of myself.

"Let's do this!" I say.

"Ok, but I want you to know that I think this is a dumb idea."

I move into position in front of the mirror again and put on my helmet.

"Ok, are you ready?" asks Fred.

"You bet. And I haven't pulled out one single wire this time," I joke to Fred when he is at the controls.

While I'm waiting for Fred to start the machine, I start posing with my bow in the mirror. I look pretty cool with my bow. I change from pose to pose. I should be a model as well as a Ninja Spy.

TWANG!

Oh man!

Not again!

My bow catches another loose wire and yanks it out of the machine.

I look around to Fred and catch his eye the moment he pulls down the lever.

"Fred-"

He sees the loose wire, but it is too late!

Fred's face is covered in disappointment. I give a grin and a shrug as the room fills with blinding light.

I look into the mirror and my reflection has disappeared again. Please be a nice version of me.

"Awe, man. We are in trouble," I hear Fred whisper.

I turn around to where I expect to find a clone but there is nothing.

"That was another important wire. It was connected to the *quantity regulator*," explains Fred.

"Connected to the what?"

"Look outside," whispers Fred as he points out the window.

I look through the window.

I squint.

I pause.

I rub my eyes.

Are you serious?!

Outside the shed there are 100 clones of me!

"This gets worse too, I dumbed this version of you down. The clever version was too hard to control," confesses Fred.

Ah great, outside my garden shed stands 100 dumb versions of me. I can also see that they all have bows. The cloning machine must have copied my weapons too.

I rush outside to address my new replicas.

"Alright listen, you lot of Ninja Spy Copy Cats! I am the original you and therefore your superior leader!" I announce.

A few seconds pass before I get a response from my army of me.

"Yes, yes of course you are right," one clone replies.

"You are the first one, so we are your servants," another replies.

"That makes sense," agrees another clone.

What?! They will just believe anything I say? How can I be so gullible? It makes me angry that this version of me even exists! They are going to give me a bad name!

"My name's Blake!" shouts one of my clones.

"Me Blake too," shouts another.

"Shh! My parents are inside the house! I don't want them to see all of you!"

"Me Blake," whispers another clone.

"I know who you guys are! You don't need to introduce yourselves," I reply.

I start to hear some bickering amongst the group.

"You look stupid."

"Me look good, you look really stupid."

"No, I'm much better looking than you two."

"You are all the same!" I snap. "You are clones!"

Oh brother. My clones are super stupid. This could be a really difficult task to take back my identity.

"Listen up team! We are off to battle a cleverer version of yourselves!"

"Can he be our leader?" asks one of my clones.

"No! I'm your leader! We need to eliminate the smarter version of me!" I yell.

"But he is a better version of you. Why not follow him?"

"Shut up! All of you!" I cut the questions short. I don't want to have an uprising against myself.

"I'm the boss! The smarter Blake is trying to kiss your girl Agent Lightning!" I'll need to trick myself into the fight.

"Me like girl!" yells one clone.

"Let's go fight me!"

Chapter 8

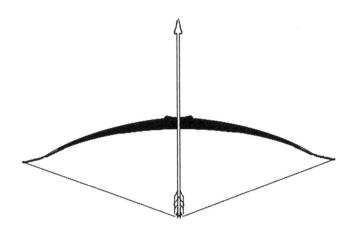

We find my clever clone and Agent Lightning at the top of Lover's Lookout. It is located on the edge of a dangerous cliff face. They are enjoying a thick shake… from the same cup! A tropical flavored thick shake! That is my flavor! Get your own flavor, Clone!

"Hey Clone!" I yell out to my copy cat. "Time is up! Time to let me be me! I will not let you destroy the Ninja Spy Agency!"

I move my body into my Ninja Spy fighting stance. My fists are tight and my legs are bent in a wide position.

"Ha ha," he laughs at me.

"Blake, what are you doing? Why is there 100 of you here?!" interrupts Agent Lightning.

"I want my life back!" I reply.

With that comment I give the signal to my army to load their bows with arrows and take aim. They all only carry one arrow each but that equals 100 arrows aimed at my clone.

"Haha, you don't scare me," chuckles my clone.

"Fire!" I give the command.

100 arrows shoot into the air towards their target. It takes me a second to realize but they have gotten their target wrong.

They have shot 100 arrows at me!

My army is full of idiots!

I preform a commando roll and hide behind a bin.

After the arrows miss me, I jump up and scream at my army.

"What are you doing!? I'm not the clone! He is over there! I am standing here on the same side as you! We just walked here together!"

"Sorry, you just look the same, and you were closer," replies one of my incompetent clones.

"Ha ha!" laughs my smarter clone. "Did you create an even dumber clone of yourself?"

"Argh! My goodness! Idiots! Just go and tackle him then," I command.

My clone army charges towards my smarter clone.

They jump him, but he is able to counter the ninja attacks. I figure the smarter version of me can easily predict what the stupid version of me is going to do.

My clever clone is hurling my other clones around like pillows!

He looks like he is enjoying it too!

Whoa! He just flipped a clone over the fence and off the cliff! And another! Now he is playing games with my army!

"Hey Blake!" yells duplicate Blake. "What's that over there?"

He points up in the air to nothing.

My stupid army all turn and look up!

How can they fall for that old trick!

Before I am able to yell out that it is a distraction, my smart clone roundhouse kicks one of my preoccupied clones.

That clone knocks another clone, who knocks another, who knocks another.

They topple off the cliff like dominos.

Ahhhh, my clone army is useless!

I'm going to need to do this myself.

I throw a left hook to my smart clone's torso.

It connects with huge force and launches him over a fence.

On the other side of the fence is a short slope, then the cliff face.

He fights back with some of my most awesome moves. We battle on the cliff's edge. My arms are aching from punching myself so much.

I flick my foot under his and slide it so he becomes off balance.

Unfortunately, my clone has the same move in mind and performs it on me!

We cause each other to tumble off the cliff!

As I bounce off the cliff, I manage to grab the edge! I barely hang on with one hand!

I look to my side and my clone has done the same thing! We are both hanging from the edge of the cliff!

Agent Lightning jumps the fence to come to our aid.

"Help me," I yell out to her. "Pull me up!"

"What?!" shouts my clone. "Don't help him! Help me!"

My hand slips a little and time is running out!

Agent Lightning can't tell who is the clone and who is the real Blake.

She has us muddled up and she only has the time to save one of us from falling.

"It's me! The real Blake! Save me!" I plead. "My clone has gone mad with power! He kidnapped my friend Fred and tied him up! He is trying to take my life and wants to destroy the Ninja Spy Agency! And if anyone objects, he will eliminate them!"

"What?! That's a pity, I kind of liked the new Blake," mumbles Agent Lightning.

"It's true," yells my clone. He must know that Agent Lightning will save me, the original. "He has gone mad with power!" he continues as he implies I'm the clone.

Argh! Am I this unbearable to everyone else?

Agent Lightning is standing above us with a very big choice - which one does she save?

Agent Lightning stands still.

She thinks for a second.

Then she pulls out her B.U.M!

Not her real bum, but the Brain Understanding Measurer!

"I'm going to use the B.U.M. to measure your brain activity. The clone will have greater brain activity on the Brain Understanding Device because he is much, much smarter!" says Agent Lightning with confidence.

She scans both our heads with her B.U.M. Her B.U.M. flashes as it scans!

"You flashed your bum!" I yell out.

Probably not a great time to make jokes.

"Ha ha, nice one," chuckles my clone.

At least we have the same sense of humor.

Agent Lightning looks at the results on the scanner. She looks at me and winks.

Ha ha! Yay! My stupidity saved me!

Agent Lightning moves across to my clone, but she is not helping him.

She kneels down.

"You have too much brain power, Mr. Copycat," says Agent Lightning, "There is only enough room on this planet for one Blake. And I like the one who doesn't want to destroy the Ninja Spy Agency."

Agent Lightning moves across to me and helps me up. And just in time, my hands were just about to slip.

"Thank you for saving me! You made the right choice," I say.

"Don't let me down Blake. No more stupid ideas like cloning yourself to avoid school," she says.

"What should we do with him?" I ask.

"Let's help him u....Hey?!" replies Agent Lightning, "He's gone!"

I look around quickly but there is no sign of him.

"He'll be back, Blake. And when he does come back, we'd better be ready to stop him."

Epilogue

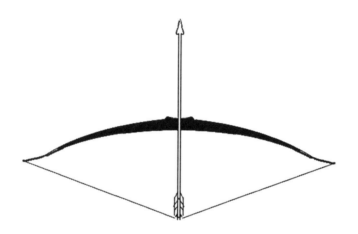

The following day, I go to Fred's house so we can walk to school together.

"We cannot mention anything of the clone incident at school. It will alert people to my secret identity as a Ninja Spy," I say to Fred at the front door.

"Not a problem," replies Fred as he hands me a piece of paper. "Here's your homework."

"Wow, thanks Fred! This must have taken ages! When did you get the time to do that?"

"I have lots of time now," Fred shrugs. "You know, maybe it was a good idea to create a clone to help complete your tasks."

"Yes it was! Thank you, Fred," I agree, walking to his front gate.

"It was just a pity you could not get along with yourself. If it wasn't for that, it would have been a great plan," continues Fred.

"But it was too dangerous. We should never do anything like that again. No more clones," I say, but then I notice something weird.

I see Fred staring at us from his house.

But Fred is still standing next to me!

No way! *Has he?* He has!

He made a clone of himself!

"Fred!" I yell out, but he runs down the street away from me.

Oh well, hopefully they are good clones…

The End

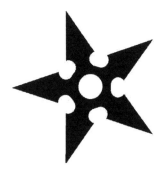

Also by William Thomas and Peter Patrick:

Diary of a Ninja Spy

Diary of a Ninja Spy 2

Diary of a Ninja Spy 3

Diary of a Ninja Spy 5

In the Diary of a Super Spy Series:

Diary of a Super Spy

Diary of a Super Spy 2: Attack of the Ninjas!

Diary of a Super Spy 3: A Giant Problem!

Diary of a Super Spy 4: Space!

Diary of a Super Spy 5: Evil Attack!

Diary of a Super Spy 6: Daylight Robbery!

Made in the USA
Middletown, DE
10 October 2020

21551888R00044